# Doggy Stage Fright

*That must be Lola's cue*, Nancy thought.

She saw Bess at the end of the runway, waving a biscuit high. Lola's ears perked up. But instead of walking toward the biscuit, she just looked at it!

The audience stared at Lola.

"Come on, Lola!" Nancy whispered. "Work it!"

Bess waved the biscuit faster and faster. George ran over to help. She snapped her fingers to get Lola to come. But Lola stood frozen, like a big white poodle statue!

Nancy gulped.

Something was wrong. Terribly wrong!

# Join the CLUE CREW
## & solve these other cases!

#1 Sleepover Sleuths

#2 Scream for Ice Cream

#3 Pony Problems

#4 The Cinderella Ballet Mystery

#5 Case of the Sneaky Snowman

#6 The Fashion Disaster

# Nancy Drew

## #6 AND THE CLUE CREW™

# The Fashion Disaster

## BY CAROLYN KEENE

### ILLUSTRATED BY MACKY PAMINTUAN

Aladdin Paperbacks
New York  London  Toronto  Sydney

This book is a work of fiction. Any references to historical events, real people, or real locales are used fictitiously. Other names, characters, places, and incidents are the product of the author's imagination, and any resemblance to actual events or locales or persons, living or dead, is entirely coincidental.

🐾 ALADDIN PAPERBACKS

An imprint of Simon & Schuster Children's Publishing Division

1230 Avenue of the Americas, New York, NY 10020

Text copyright © 2007 by Simon & Schuster, Inc.

Illustrations copyright © 2007 by Macky Pamintuan

All rights reserved, including the right of reproduction in whole or in part in any form.

ALADDIN PAPERBACKS, NANCY DREW AND THE CLUE CREW, and colophon are trademarks of Simon & Schuster, Inc.

NANCY DREW is a registered trademark of Simon & Schuster, Inc.

Designed by Lisa Vega

The text of this book was set in ITC Stone Informal.

Manufactured in the United States of America

First Aladdin Paperbacks edition February 2007

10 9 8 7 6 5 4 3

Library of Congress Control Number 2006929352

ISBN-13: 978-1-4169-3485-1

ISBN-10: 1-4169-3485-5

# CONTENTS

CHAPTER ONE: PAMPERED PUP · · · · · · · · · · · · · 1

CHAPTER TWO: DIVA DOG SHOCKER · · · · · · · · · · · 12

CHAPTER THREE: SNEAKY SWITCHEROO · · · · · · · · · · 21

CHAPTER FOUR: TRAILER BARK · · · · · · · · · · · · · 27

CHAPTER FIVE: CLOTHES CALL · · · · · · · · · · · · 35

CHAPTER SIX: PIECE BY PIECE · · · · · · · · · · · · 41

CHAPTER SEVEN: BACKPACK ATTACK · · · · · · · · · · 47

CHAPTER EIGHT: IT'S A MATCH! · · · · · · · · · · · · 54

CHAPTER NINE: "NEWFIE . . . GOOFY!" · · · · · · · · · · 63

CHAPTER TEN: HAPPILY EVER AFTER · · · · · · · · · 74

# ChaPTER ONE

## Pampered Pup

"It's like a real, live fashion show!" eight-year-old Nancy Drew said to her two best friends.

Bess Marvin and George Fayne smiled and looked down at a pug dog on a leash. He was dressed in striped overalls and matching doggy booties.

"Except in *this* fashion show the models have four legs instead of two." Bess giggled.

It was Saturday, the day of the Cool Canines Fashion Show in River Heights Park. Mr. Drew had driven the girls to the park and agreed to meet them by the fashion show stage before showtime. Nancy was extra excited because her Labrador puppy, Chocolate Chip, was a model in the show.

"Isn't Chip totally stylin' in her doggy denim outfit?" Nancy asked. "It's from the Funky Fido Boutique."

George bent down to straighten Chip's cap. "Chip looks totally fetching," she said. "Fetch . . . dog . . . get it?"

Bess rolled her blue eyes. "That's the fifth dog joke today, George," she said. "One more and I'll start calling you Georgia!"

"No, thank you!" George said, tossing her dark curls. She hated being called by her real name.

As the girls walked through the park, Nancy couldn't believe her eyes. The park looked so festive! Colorful balloons fluttered from a long runway built just for the fashion show.

"Do you think dogs like wearing clothes?" George asked. She was more into booting up computers than picking out new boots. But her cousin Bess was the total opposite.

"Who doesn't like new clothes?" Bess asked. She twirled to show off her yellow jeans and daisy print top. "Check out my new spring outfit."

"It's nice," Nancy said. "But aren't you afraid of getting dog hairs on it?"

"Dog hairs? I laugh at dog hairs!" Bess said. She reached into her pocket and pulled out a hairbrush. It was wrapped with tape, sticky side up.

"What is that?" George asked.

"It's my Hairy Fairy Wand!" Bess said. "I built it to pick up dog and cat hairs from clothes and furniture."

"Sweet!" Nancy said. She was proud of her two friends. Bess could build or fix anything. George was a computer whiz and proud of it. All three of them were great at solving mysteries. They had even started their own detective club called the Clue Crew. But today wouldn't be about cracking cases. It would be about walking on the runway!

"Look!" George said. "There's something you don't see every day."

Nancy turned to see where George was pointing. A bright-pink trailer was parked under a tree. Written on the side in fancy silver letters was the name LOLA.

"Isn't Lola that poodle who models for cards and calendars?" Bess asked. "The one they call the Diva Dog?"

"That's the one," Nancy said. "I heard Lola's the star of the fashion show today."

"That's *superstar*!" a voice piped up.

Nancy's reddish blond hair whipped in the air as she spun around. She saw two girls standing there, and sitting on the ground between them was Lola—the famous Diva Dog!

The big white poodle was dressed in a pink chiffon skirt and cape fastened with a pearl collar. She also wore a sparkly tiara on her furry head.

"It's Lola!" George exclaimed.

"May I pet her?" Nancy asked.

"Don't even think of it," said one of the girls,

who had wavy blond hair. "Lola just had a raw
egg shampoo!"

"And a manicure!" the other, red-haired girl
said. "Don't forget about the manicure, Maya."

"Like, duh, Nicki!" Maya groaned. "I'm the

one who picked out her cotton-candy pink nail polish, remember?"

Nancy glanced down at Lola's paws. The poodle really *was* wearing pink nail polish!

"Lola is *my* dog," Maya said. "My parents let me take her to fashion shows, photo shoots, pawtograph signings—"

"Pawtograph?" Nancy asked.

"Lola signs her pictures with her paw print," Nicki explained. "You know, autographs . . . pawtographs."

Maya and Nicki introduced themselves. They were in the third grade, just like Nancy, Bess, and George. The girls lived in the next town, Valley View.

"My name is Nancy," Nancy said. She pointed to Bess and George. "And these are my friends—"

*BZZZZZZ!*

The noise made Nancy jump. It came from Nicki's watch.

"Twelve fifteen," Nicki said. "Time for Lola's vitamin water break!"

Nicki pulled a bottle of water from her purple backpack and put it to Lola's mouth. She held it steady as Lola slurped loudly.

"Nicki is Lola's personal assistant," Maya whispered. "She can't have her own dog because her brother is allergic. So being around Lola is the next best thing."

Just then a gray, fuzzy-faced dog scampered over. He was wearing an orange vest that read "Adopt Me." Nancy guessed the dog came from the Rollover Rescue Shelter. The shelter had set up a tent in the park for the day.

Chip and the dog touched noses. But when the fuzzy-faced pup walked toward Lola, Maya screamed, "A shelter dog! Get him away from Lola! Get him away!"

ADOPT
ME

The little gray dog scooted in and out between Nancy, Bess, and George's legs. The girls laughed and shrieked.

"Percy! Sit! Stay! Heel! Cool your jets!" A boy wearing an orange T-shirt ran over. Nancy thought he looked about nine years old. The boy tried to catch Percy but with no luck.

"We've got him!" a voice called.

Two teenagers wearing the same orange shirts as the boy raced over. Nancy read their name tags. The teenagers were Tracey and Vincent. The younger boy's name was Rusty.

Tracey pointed her finger at Percy. Then, in a firm voice, she said, "Sit!"

Percy stopped in his tracks and sat down, just like magic!

"Good boy," Vincent said.

"Wow!" Nancy said. "You guys are great with dogs!"

"That's because we're the Bow-Wow Brigade," Vincent said with a smile. "We volunteer for the Rollover Rescue Shelter. We feed dogs, walk them, clean their cages—"

"Ew!" Bess put in. "I hate cleaning out the hamster cage at school."

"I don't mind," Rusty said. "Before this, I volunteered at another pet shelter in Valley View."

"Valley View?" Maya said. "There is no pet shelter in my town. And no shelter dogs, either!"

"Huh?" Rusty said, wrinkling his nose.

"What's wrong with shelter dogs?" Vincent asked.

"The dogs we rescue are great," Tracey said.

"They're okay, if you like mutts and junkyard dogs," Maya said. "My Lola is a purebred standard poodle from the south of France!"

"Yeah . . . and I'm Spider-Man," Rusty muttered.

The Bow-Wow Brigade and Percy walked away. Nancy could tell they didn't like what Maya said about shelter dogs.

"We'd better go too," Nancy said. "Chip is

in the fashion show later, and I'm walking her down the runway."

"Lola walks down the runway all by herself," Maya bragged. "As long as Nicki waves her favorite dog biscuit."

"Chip has a favorite biscuit too," Nancy said. "It's called Lick My Chops."

"Shh!" Maya hissed. "Don't mention those yucky biscuits in front of Lola. She hates them!"

"Lola only eats Bone Appetit biscuits," Nicki said. "They're from a fancy pet bakery in New York City."

Nicki pulled a biscuit from her purple backpack. Nancy, Bess, and George jumped back. The biscuit smelled like stinky cheese!

"Lola's favorite flavor is blue cheese and onions," Maya explained. "She can smell them a mile away!"

George squeezed her nose and said, "So can we."

"Here. Give this to Lola," Nicki said. She tossed a biscuit to Bess. "Then you can tell everyone you fed the famous Diva Dog!"

Bess scrunched her nose as she caught the stinky biscuit. "That's okay," she said. "I don't really have to—"

"Arrf!" Lola jumped at the biscuit, her paws landing on Bess's shoulders.

"Lola—no!" Nicki said.

Nancy gasped. Bess's brand-new daisy top was covered with muddy paw prints!

# ChaPTER TWO

## Diva Dog Shocker

"Oh, no!" Bess cried as Lola jumped down, crunching the biscuit. "My new daisy top!"

"Are you lucky or what?" Maya said. "Now you'll have Lola's pawtograph all over your shirt!"

Nancy couldn't believe her ears! "Lucky?" she said. "Bess's new shirt is ruined."

"And Lola has the worst dog breath I ever smelled in my life," Bess muttered.

"Lola didn't mean it," Maya said with a smile. "But I know how I can make it up to you."

"How?" Bess asked glumly.

"Why don't you wave Lola's dog biscuit in the fashion show today?" Maya said.

"But I thought that was Nicki's job," Bess said.

"It *is* my job!" Nicki agreed.

"Not today, Nicki," Maya told her.

Nicki's face turned about as red as her hair.

"Fine!" she snapped. "I am sick of being a maid to that diva dog, anyway. Whatever Lola wants—Lola gets!"

Chip barked after Nicki as she stormed off.

"Nicki said 'diva' like it was a bad thing," Maya said with a shrug. She turned to Bess. "Well? Will you do it?"

"I don't know," Bess said slowly.

"Go for it, Bess!" George exclaimed.

"You'll get to be in the fashion show," Nancy said. "Just like Chip and me."

Bess's eyes lit up. Finally she smiled and said, "Okay. I'm in."

"Neat!" Maya said. "Lola's Bon Appetit biscuits are in a basket inside her trailer. My mom and dad filled it with fresh ones about a half hour ago."

"Are your parents in the trailer?" Nancy asked.

"No," Maya said. "They're at the mayor's lunch party in the park rec hall right now."

"My mom is there too!" George said. "She's a caterer. She cooked veggie lasagna and double-chocolate brownies for the party. I hope she brings home a doggy bag."

"Was that another dog joke?" Bess groaned.

Maya waved good-bye as she walked off with Lola.

Suddenly the loudspeaker crackled and an announcement blared. The fashion show would begin at one o'clock sharp.

"It's twelve thirty now," Nancy said, glancing at her watch. "We'd better pick up those biscuits."

"What if I can't find them?" Bess asked.

"You will," George said. "Just follow the smell!"

On the way to Lola's trailer, the girls saw kids from their school, River Heights Elementary. Ned Nickerson was walking his German shepherd, Max. Kevin Garcia was there with his beagle, Hudson. Andrea Wu was trying to stop her terrier, Angus, from chasing a squirrel.

But when the girls saw Peter Patino they had to stop and stare. Peter was walking a gigantic dog with thick black fur. A string of drool hung from the dog's mouth.

"Is that your dog, Peter?" Nancy called.

Peter stopped to give the dog a biscuit. "It's Mayor Strong's dog, Huey," he called back. "I'm just walking him while the mayor has his lunch party—whoaaaaa!"

The dog barked as he dragged Peter away.

"It looks like Huey is walking Peter!" Nancy giggled.

The girls stopped to watch a clown make balloon animals in the shape of poodles. Then they remembered the biscuits, and they raced to the pink trailer and filed inside.

"Check out this place!" Nancy exclaimed.

Pinned to the wall were fashion photos of Lola. A fancy brass dog bed stood against the wall. Racks and shelves were filled with canine clothes and accessories. There was even a frilly vanity table that held bottles of doggy perfume!

"Now *this* is a doghouse!" George said.

"There's the basket!" said Bess. She ran to a brown basket that stood on a small table. Inside the basket were three dog biscuits. Nancy held Chip back as the puppy jumped at the treats.

"They don't smell so bad this time," Bess said. "Must be a different flavor."

George pointed to a sticky-looking puddle on the floor right next to the table. "Don't step in that," she said.

"Ew," Bess said, looking down. "I guess even diva dogs can have accidents!"

The girls left the trailer and ran straight to the fashion show runway. They checked in by the stage with Mr. Drew, and then Nancy and Chip lined up with the other owners and their dogs. Nancy saw a bulldog dressed as a cow-boy, a dachshund wearing a leather jacket with silver studs, and even a Chihuahua in a hula skirt. But sitting like a princess at the front of the line was Lola the Diva Dog!

"Don't worry, Chip," Nancy whispered. "You'll always be top dog to me."

She was petting Chip when Mayor Strong and a woman walked by. Nancy recognized the woman with the dark hair and bright-red lipstick. Her name was

Patsy Ray, and she owned the Funky Fido Boutique.

"I still can't believe Lola is wearing that outfit," Patsy said in an angry voice. "I wanted her to wear one of my designs!"

"And I already explained it to you, Patsy," Mayor Strong said. "I promised Lola's owners she could wear an outfit from her new calendar."

Patsy's bone-shaped earrings swung back and forth as she shook her head. "Big mistake!" she said. "My clothes are so much cuter."

Then Patsy turned on her high heel and walked away.

*Wow*, Nancy thought. *And they call Lola a diva!*

Mayor Strong walked up the steps to the runway. The crowd cheered. Nancy's tummy fluttered like a million butterflies. She saw her dad out in the audience. It was showtime!

"I'm sure you're all excited to see Lola strut her stuff," Mayor Strong said with a smile. "But first let's welcome another superstar, Broadway actress Lorette Waters!"

Lorette waved as she joined the mayor on stage. "Thank you, Mayor Strong," she said. "Thank you, River Heights!"

Nancy listened as Lorette spoke about the importance of adopting homeless shelter dogs. Next the actress sang a song she'd written herself called "Send in the Hounds." As Lorette belted out the last stanza, she turned dramatically toward Lola.

*That must be Lola's cue*, Nancy thought.

She saw Bess at the end of the runway, waving a biscuit high. Lola's ears perked up. But instead of walking toward the biscuit, she just looked at it!

The audience stared at Lola.

"Come on, Lola!" Nancy whispered. "Work it!"

Bess waved the biscuit faster and faster. George ran over to help. She snapped her fingers to get Lola to come. But Lola stood frozen, like a big white poodle statue!

Nancy gulped.

Something was wrong. Terribly wrong!

# ChaPTER ThReE

## Sneaky Switcheroo

"Some diva dog!" Patsy Ray laughed from the stage. She was helping Lorette announce the show. "She can't even fetch a biscuit!"

Nancy frowned. Patsy Ray wasn't being very nice.

"Oh, well, folks," Lorette announced, "I guess even dogs get stage fright sometimes."

"Not this dog!" Maya shouted as she raced toward the runway. "Lola is a pro. A superstar!"

Maya grabbed the biscuit from Bess. She waved it herself—until she looked at it and shrieked.

"Waaaaa! This isn't a Bone Appetit biscuit, it's Lick My Chops!" Maya dropped the biscuit

21

back into the basket and pointed to Bess. "And *she* switched the dog biscuits!"

"What?" Bess gasped.

Nancy was so surprised that she dropped Chip's leash. Chip barked and raced toward the basket of Lick My Chops biscuits. All the other dogs charged down the runway for the biscuits too—all the dogs except Lola!

"Angus, come back!" Andrea called.

"Hudson—bad dog!" Kevin shouted.

Dogs barked and whined as their owners

ran to catch them. Nancy had to jump over a dachshund to get at Chip.

"I didn't switch any biscuits!" Bess said over the noisy dogs and shouting owners. "I didn't!"

Nancy grabbed Chip's leash. She saw two grown-ups standing next to Maya. They had blond hair like Maya's.

"Mom, Dad, I know Bess did it," Maya said. "Lola jumped on her with muddy paws. So Bess got even by replacing the biscuits with the kind Lola hates!"

"You made that up, Maya!" George exclaimed.

"George and I were in the trailer when Bess picked up the biscuits," Nancy said. "She didn't switch anything."

"You're Bess's best friends," Maya said. "You probably *helped* her switch the biscuits!"

"We did not!" Nancy said.

Mayor Strong formed the letter *T* with his hands. "Time-out, everybody," he said. "Why don't we get some of Lola's favorite biscuits so she'll walk down the runway?"

"Because I don't want Lola in the fashion show anymore," Maya said.

"What?" the mayor cried.

"Lola is Maya's dog," Maya's mother said.

"So it's her call," added Maya's dad.

"But Mr. and Mrs. Milton," Mayor Strong reasoned. "All these people came to see Lola the Diva Dog!"

"They did not!" Patsy argued. "They came to see my fashions!"

"They came to adopt shelter dogs!" Lorette said.

"Can't we just have a fashion show?" George groaned.

The dogs and their owners lined up again—minus Lola. Nancy could see Lola's trailer zooming away. She couldn't believe Maya had accused all three of them of switching the biscuits!

"And now, after a little excitement," Mayor Strong announced, "the First Annual Cool Canines Fashion Show!"

Nancy tried not to think about Maya as she walked Chip down the runway.

"This is Chocolate Chip," Patsy said into the microphone, "looking cookie-sweet in her denim doggy ensemble—on sale now at the Funky Fido Boutique!"

The fashion show was a success even without Lola. Ned's dog Max needed some coaxing, but he walked down the runway like a pro. Andrea's dog got lots of laughs. And big Huey left a puddle of sticky drool on the runway.

When the show was over, Nancy ran over to Bess and George. They were helping Mrs. Fayne load her catering van. "That was fun, wasn't it?" Nancy asked.

"Fun?" George snorted.

"First my daisy top gets ruined," Bess said. "Now everyone thinks we switched those dumb dog biscuits!"

"No," Nancy said, shaking her head. "Just because Maya thinks that doesn't mean everybody does."

Just then two boys rode by on their scooters. One pointed at Nancy, Bess, and George.

"Hey, there they are!" one boy shouted. "Those are the girls who switched the dog biscuits!"

"Sneaky, sneaky, sneaky," the other said.

As the boys scooted away, Bess heaved a big sigh and said, "See what I mean?"

"Now what are we going to do?" George asked.

Nancy thought for a moment. There was only one thing for them to do. . . .

"We have to find out who really switched Lola's dog biscuits," she said.

"We?" Bess asked.

"As in the Clue Crew?" George chimed in.

"Sure," Nancy said with a smile. "We always help others by solving mysteries. It's time to help *ourselves*!"

# CHAPTER FOUR

## Trailer Bark

"Good morning!" Nancy said as she walked into the kitchen on Sunday.

"Morning, Sleeping Beauty!" Mr. Drew said. He was washing strawberries at the kitchen sink. Hannah Gruen was placing a plate of pancakes on the table.

Hannah had been the Drews' housekeeper from the time Nancy was three years old. She had helped take care of Nancy ever since her mother died.

Nancy smiled when she saw the yummy pancakes. But when she glanced at the Sunday newspaper on the table, she gasped. Splashed

across the front page was the headline FAMOUS
DIVA DOG FLIPS AT FASHION SHOW!

"Lola!" Nancy said.

"I read about that diva dog," Hannah said.
"Why do you think she froze like that?"

"Somebody switched Lola's favorite dog biscuits on purpose," Nancy said. "The Clue Crew
is going to find out who did it."

Mr. Drew popped a strawberry into Nancy's
mouth. He was a lawyer and sometimes helped

his daughter with her cases. "Sounds like an important case," he said. "Where are you going to start?"

Nancy caught a whiff of the pancakes and answered, "With a good breakfast, Daddy. Pass the maple syrup, please!"

After breakfast, Bess and George rang the doorbell. Then the Clue Crew ran up the stairs two at a time to Nancy's room, which was also Clue Crew Detective Headquarters.

"Okay. Let's get to work," Nancy declared.

George sat behind Nancy's computer. Her hands flew across the keyboard as she opened up a file for the case.

Bess plopped down on Nancy's bed. She tossed a stuffed unicorn up and down in the air. Throwing stuffed animals around was how she did her best thinking.

"First, let's come up with a time line," Nancy said. "When do you think Lola's biscuits were switched?"

"Maya said her parents had just filled the

basket with biscuits right before the lunch party," George remembered. "And the lunch party started at noon."

"If the party was at noon yesterday," Nancy said, "and we got to Lola's trailer a few minutes before the show—"

"Which started at one o'clock!" Bess cut in.

"That means," Nancy continued, "that the biscuits were switched between twelve and one o'clock."

"Write that down, George!" Bess said.

"What do you think I'm doing, Bess?" George joked as she typed. "Playing the piano?"

"Now that we have a time line, what about suspects?" Nancy asked. "Who would want to spoil Lola's big moment?"

"Probably someone who doesn't like Lola," Bess said. She began tossing a stuffed kangaroo in the air. "Or doesn't like Maya."

"What about Nicki?" Nancy said. "She was mad at Maya for giving her job to Bess."

"But where would Nicki get Lick My Chops

dog biscuits?" George asked. "She doesn't even have a dog."

"And all she fed Lola was that stinky kind," Bess said.

"Nicki had to get the Lick My Chops biscuits from somewhere," Nancy said. "In the meantime, she's a suspect."

George typed "Suspects," and underneath she wrote Nicki's name. Then Chip padded into the room. She was wearing the denim cap from the fashion show the day before.

"Chip looks so cute in Patsy's clothes!" Bess giggled.

"Patsy!" Nancy remembered. "She was arguing with Mayor Strong yesterday because Lola wasn't wearing the clothes she designed."

"Maybe Patsy switched Lola's biscuits," Bess said. "To make Lola look bad."

"Patsy Ray," George declared as she typed. "Suspect number two!"

"Two suspects but zero clues," Nancy said. "I wish we could go back and search Lola's trailer."

"How?" Bess asked. "We don't even know where to find it!"

"That's what *you* think!" George said.

She went online. After a bit of typing, Lola's own website came up. There was a picture of the poodle, surrounded by pink and silver stars. George clicked on the star marked "Meet Lola!" A page opened up, showing a list of Lola's appearances.

"Lola is signing pawtographs at the new pet store on River Street," George said. "Today at eleven-thirty!"

"Her trailer might be parked there too," Nancy said. "River Street, here we come!"

The girls each had the same rule: They could walk up to five blocks away from any of their houses, as long as they walked together and asked permission. River Street was less than five blocks away, so they were in luck!

When the three friends reached River Street, they spotted Lola's trailer. It was parked outside the new pet store, Ruffs and Meows.

Nancy, Bess, and George peeked through the store window. They saw Maya standing with Lola as kids lined up for her pawtograph.

Maya's mom stood outside. She was busy talking to a news reporter and a cameraperson. Lola's trailer was just a few feet away.

"The door is open," Nancy whispered. "Let's go!"

The girls slipped quietly into the trailer. Once inside, they scurried around looking for clues.

George studied the table where the basket used to be.

"If someone did switch the biscuits," she said, "what would they do with the Bone Appetits?"

"Maybe throw them away," Nancy guessed. She looked inside a small trash can, where she found shreds of paper.

"Somebody ripped up a note," she said. "That could be a clue."

Nancy never went anywhere without a pocket-size spyglass and plastic bags for her clues. She pulled a bag out of her pocket and filled it with the paper shreds.

"Look!" Bess said. She pointed to a framed picture on the wall. "It's Maya holding a poodle puppy. I'll bet it's Lola's baby picture!"

"We don't have time for that, Bess," George said. "We have to look for clues before—"

"—Mom!" a voice called from outside.

The girls froze.

It was Maya!

"I'm just going inside the trailer to get something, Mom," Maya's voice said next.

"Oh, no!" Bess gasped. "She's coming!"

"What do we do?" George whispered.

"We have to hide," Nancy said. "Right now!"

# CHAPTER FIVE

## Clothes Call

"Hide? Where?" George said.

The girls quickly looked around the trailer. Nancy spotted a large wire dog crate. Draped over it was a satiny blanket.

"Lola's crate," Nancy whispered. "There's room in there for all of us!"

"Gross!" Bess groaned.

The girls crawled inside.

Nancy gulped as she sat on a rubber steak dog toy that squeaked. George reached out to drape the cloth over the front of the crate. The girls held their breaths as the trailer door creaked open.

Nancy could hear Maya walking into the

trailer. She also heard a *click-click* sound—like dog paws on tiles.

"What a time to run out of pictures, Lola," Maya said. "Now where did I put your latest publicity photos?"

The girls were twisted inside the crate like pretzels. They heard Maya moving stuff around. Suddenly the *click-click-click* noise got louder and louder—as if Lola was walking toward the crate!

*Back, Lola, back*, Nancy thought.

Lola popped her head under the blanket and into the crate.

"Oh, noooo," Bess groaned.

After sniffing Bess's elbow and Nancy's sneakers, she began licking George's face!

George squeezed her eyes and mouth shut as Lola's tongue washed her face. Nancy hoped that George wouldn't yell out. But then Lola began licking George's mouth.

"Yuck! Ick! Phooey!" George yelled, wiping her mouth with both hands.

"Woof!" Lola barked.

One by one the girls spilled out of the crate. Maya stared at them as if they were from outer space.

"What are you doing here?" she demanded.

Nancy, Bess, and George all spoke at once.

"We're detectives!"

"We were looking for clues!"

37

"And the real person who switched the dog biscuits—"

"MOM!" Maya shouted.

"Maya—no!" Nancy said. "We can explain!"

Maya's mom peeked into the trailer.

"Guess what, honey?" she asked. "A nice television reporter wants to interview you with Lola. It's for the six o'clock news on WRIV-TV!"

"TV?" Maya said. A smile spread across her face.

"What should I tell them?" her mom asked.

"Tell them we're ready for our close-up!" Maya declared. She threw back her shoulders. Then she and Lola marched out of the trailer.

"I think I've seen you girls before," Maya's mom said. "Aren't you—"

"Lola's biggest fans!" George cut in.

"And we were just leaving," Nancy added.

"Bye-bye," Bess said.

The girls bumped into one another as they squeezed through the trailer door. As they ran down River Street, Nancy glanced over her shoulder. Maya was happily chatting to the reporter.

"That was close!" Nancy said when they slowed down. She pulled the plastic bag with the paper pieces from her pocket. "But we did pick up this clue."

"And dog hairs!" Bess said. She pulled out her Hairy Fairy Wand and swept it across their clothes. "I knew this would come in handy someday."

The girls talked about the case as they walked down River Street. With all its stores and places to eat, it was the busiest street in River Heights.

A woman walked by carrying a Funky Fido Boutique shopping bag.

"The Funky Fido Boutique is open today," Nancy said. "Let's go there and question Patsy."

The boutique was just down the block. Its window was filled with all kinds of dog clothes and accessories—sailor suits, hats, even angel wings!

"I don't get it," Bess said. "Why would someone

who designs such sweet dog clothes do something so mean?"

"She did say mean things about Lola," said George.

"Yeah, and I just thought of something," Nancy added.

"What?" Bess asked.

Nancy stared at her friends and said, "What if Patsy is mean to *us*?"

# ChaPTER Six

## Piece by Piece

"May I help you?" Patsy asked. Her back was to the girls as she hung fashion sketches on the wall. They were of dogs wearing ballet costumes.

"Why are those dogs wearing tutus?" George asked.

"I'm designing costumes for a doggy ballet called *The Muttcracker*," Patsy said. She turned around and peered over her red-framed glasses.

"Weren't you and your little dog in the fashion show yesterday?" Patsy asked Nancy.

Nancy gulped as she nodded. Then she gathered her courage and got right down to business.

"Patsy, do you remember when Lola wouldn't

walk down the runway yesterday?" Nancy asked.

"How could I forget?" Patsy said. "I laughed so hard my contact lens almost popped out."

The girls traded looks. Patsy was still saying mean things about Lola!

"Do you think you know who switched the biscuits?" Nancy asked Patsy.

"How should I know?" Patsy said with a shrug.

George stepped forward. "Then maybe you know where you were between twelve and one o'clock yesterday afternoon!" she said.

Patsy blinked hard. Then she smiled and said, "I'll take a wild guess. You girls are playing detective, right?"

"We're not playing, Ms. Ray," Nancy said.

"We *are* detectives," Bess added. "We're the Clue Crew!"

"You just gave me a super idea," Patsy said. She grabbed a sketchbook and began drawing on a fresh page. "I'll design detective clothes for dogs. Like tiny trench coats and those tweedy Sherlock Holmes caps—"

"Ms. Ray, please," Nancy cut in. "Can you tell us where you were yesterday?"

"Okay, let's see," said Patsy. "Yesterday between twelve o'clock and one o'clock I was at the mayor's lunch party. That's it."

Patsy turned back to her sketching. The girls began to whisper.

"She's acting like this is a big joke," Bess complained. "How do we know she's telling the truth about the mayor's lunch party?"

"I have an idea!" George declared.

She walked up to Patsy and said, "Ms. Ray? Do you recall what you ate at Mayor Strong's lunch party on Saturday between twelve and one o'clock?"

Patsy smiled for the first time, a big, bright smile.

"Sure do!" Patsy said. "I had the most fabulous vegetable lasagna. And for dessert I ate these scrumptious chocolate brownies. Double chocolate, I think."

"Vegetable lasagna and chocolate brownies are correct!" George declared.

Nancy smiled too. Patsy *was* at the lunch party. So she couldn't have been in the trailer switching the biscuits!

"I'll tell my mom you liked the food, Ms. Ray," George said. "She cooked all of it, you know."

"Your mom is a very good cook," Patsy said. Then she added with a wink, "And you girls are *awesome* detectives."

"Thank you!" Nancy, Bess, and George said together.

Maybe Patsy wasn't so mean after all!

The girls thanked Patsy and left the Funky Fido Boutique.

"Now our only suspect is Nicki," Bess said. "And we don't have a clue where she is."

"Clue!" Nancy gasped. "I almost forgot!"

She pulled the plastic bag from her pocket. Inside were the torn-up pieces of paper from the trash can.

"Let's put this note together and see what it says," Nancy suggested. "Maybe it'll give us some more leads."

The girls ran to an empty table in front of a café. Nancy poured the pieces out on the table. In a flash the girls were working at putting them together.

"It's just like a jigsaw puzzle!" Bess said.

As the pieces came together, George read the first words out loud: "MAYA . . . WE . . . KNOW . . . YOUR . . . SE."

"Se . . . Se . . ."

Bess thought out loud. "We know your seal! Your seahorse! Your set of crayons!"

George added the letter C.

"Sec . . . sec . . . secretary!" Bess shouted. "We know your *secretary*!"

"Bess," George complained. "Wait until all the pieces are together."

Nancy matched the last pieces:

R . . . E . . . T.

Then she read the message out loud: "MAYA. WE KNOW YOUR SECRET."

The girls traded looks. Secret? What secret?

# ChaPTER SEVEN

## Backpack Attack

"Maybe Maya's secret is something embarrassing," George said the next day. "Maybe she still sleeps with a teddy bear or something."

Bess planted her hands on her hips. "I sleep with a teddy bear!" she said. "And a dolphin, and a stuffed kitty with ruby eyes."

"Okay," George said. "Then maybe she bites her toenails."

"Ew," Bess said. "That I don't do!"

The girls were in the school yard for recess. But they weren't playing tag or kickball or swinging on the swings. They were trying to figure out the mysterious note. Nancy had taped it together when she got home the night before.

"The paper is orange with a dog paw-print design around the edges," Nancy said. "Whoever wrote it might like dogs."

"Nicki likes dogs," Bess pointed out. "And she probably knows some of Maya's secrets, too."

A ball rolled over. Nancy kicked it back to the kickball game. A girl wearing an orange T-shirt waved thanks.

Nancy's eyes flew open. The shirt made her remember the Bow-Wow Brigade. They wore orange T-shirts too!

"You guys," Nancy said, "didn't Maya say mean things about shelter dogs to the Bow-Wow Brigade?"

"Yeah!" Bess said. "Maybe they switched Lola's dog biscuits to get even."

"And while they were switching the biscuits," George added, "one of them might have stopped to write the mysterious note!"

"But what is Maya's secret?" Nancy wondered.

The end-of-recess bell rang. Nancy carefully folded the note and put it in her pocket. Then the girls lined up with the rest of their class. Their friends Nadine Nardo and Kendra Jackson stood in front of them in the line.

"Hi, Kendra," Nancy said. "Hi, Nadine."

Kendra and Nadine spun around to face Nancy. But they didn't say hi back. Instead they glared at the girls with squinty eyes.

"What's up?" George asked.

"We heard about it during recess," Nadine said. "How could you do that to Lola?"

"How could you switch her biscuits before the big fashion show?" Kendra asked. "That is so mean!"

Nancy couldn't believe it. Now their friends were blaming them for the biscuit brouhaha too!

"We didn't do it," Nancy insisted.

Kendra and Nadine hooked arms. With a huff they walked to the front of the line.

"Great," George groaned. "If we don't find out who switched those biscuits, we'll lose all our friends!"

Now Peter stood in front of the girls. He turned around and said hello.

"Hi, Peter," Nancy said. "Are you ever going to walk Huey again?"

Peter's eyes flew wide open. "Huey?" he asked. "Why do you want to know?"

"Just curious," said Nancy.

The line began to move. As they filed into the building, Nancy whispered to Bess and George, "Why was Peter acting so nervous?"

"Are you kidding?" George said. "You'd be nervous too if you had to walk a dog like Huey!"

The rest of the school day was busy with math, art, and social studies. But after three o'clock the Clue Crew was back on the case.

"Why is Chip coming with us to the Rollover Rescue Shelter, Nancy?" Bess asked.

Nancy held Chip's leash as they walked away from the Drew house. The girls had gotten permission to go to the Rollover Rescue Shelter after school.

"Because I have to walk Chip anyway,"

Nancy said. "Besides, since they like dogs so much, the Bow-Wow Brigade might be nicer to us if we have one!"

A rattling noise made Chip's ears perk up. Nancy turned and saw a girl riding a bicycle down the street. As she rode closer, Nancy could see who it was.

"It's Nicki," she said.

"Are we lucky or what?" George whispered.

"Nicki, stop!" Bess called, waving her arms.

Nicki smiled as she slowed down. Her purple backpack was stuffed in her bicycle basket. The strap from the bag dangled over the side.

"You guys were in the park on Saturday," Nicki said. "What's up?"

"We're trying to find out who switched Lola's dog biscuits at the show," Nancy said. "Maybe you can help us."

"Sorry," Nicki said. Her helmet wiggled as she shook her head. "I have no idea who did it."

Chip suddenly jumped up. She caught the strap of Nicki's backpack between her teeth.

"Chip—no!" Nancy scolded.

Too late. Chip pulled Nicki's backpack out of the basket. Stuff spilled out as it tumbled to the sidewalk. Nancy noticed a wad of gum stuck to a tissue, a dollar bill, a pencil with a

ladybug eraser, and a plastic comb.

"Sorry," Nancy said. But as she picked up the backpack, three more things fell out.

Three dog biscuits!

# ChaPTER EighT

## It's a Match!

Nancy grabbed Chip's collar as she lunged for the biscuits. They looked just like Lick My Chops!

"Where did you get those?" Nancy asked.

"They must be from Saturday," Nicki said calmly. "I forgot to clean out my backpack as usual."

"But they're Lick My Chops," Nancy pointed out. "When you fed Lola you only fed her the fancy kind."

"Those weren't for Lola," explained Nicki. "After I told Maya I quit, I went to the Roll-over Rescue tent to volunteer. Tracey gave me a bunch of biscuits to feed the shelter dogs."

Nancy watched Chip crunch the biscuits on the sidewalk. They were Lick My Chops all right!

"You can keep the biscuits." Nicki sighed. "I still don't have a dog."

Nicki adjusted her helmet and pedaled away. The girls stared down the block as she disappeared around a corner.

"How do we know she was telling the truth?" Nancy wondered.

"Too bad we don't have a lie-detector machine," George said.

"Maybe I can build one," Bess said. "Or invent a shampoo that makes a liar's hair turn green!"

"Thanks, Bess," Nancy said. "But we still have other suspects to question."

"The Bow-Wow Brigade!" Bess and George said together.

The Clue Crew went straight to the Rollover Rescue Shelter. Once inside they saw volunteers in orange T-shirts busy at work. They were walking dogs, cleaning cages, and showing adoptable dogs to possible owners.

Tracey and Vincent were there. When they saw the girls and Chip, they walked over.

"A brand-new puppy just came in," Tracey said.

"He's a schnoodle," Vincent said.

"A schnoodle?" Nancy asked.

"Part schnauzer, part poodle," Tracey explained. "Would you like to meet him?"

Nancy was curious about the schnoodle. But she shook her head and said, "We came to find out who switched Lola's dog biscuits before the fashion show."

Nancy pulled the note out of her pocket. She held it up and said, "We found this note in Lola's trailer. Did any of you write it?"

Tracey and Vincent stared at the note.

"That is our stationery," Tracey said. "But I didn't write it."

"Me neither," said Vincent with a shrug. Then he pointed to a desk. "If you'd like to volunteer, just write your name on the sign-in sheet and we'll put you to work."

The teenagers turned and walked away.

"Sign-in sheet," Nancy said. "That's it!"

"Don't tell me you want to volunteer now," George said. "We have a case to solve."

"And I'm *not* cleaning out any cages!" Bess said.

"You'll see," Nancy whispered. She waved her friends over to the desk. Then she ran her finger down the sign-in list until she found Tracey's and Vincent's signatures.

"What are you doing, Nancy?" Bess asked.

"Comparing the note to Tracey's and Vincent's signatures," Nancy explained. She held the note against the names and heaved a sigh. "The handwritings don't match."

"Somebody had to write that note," George said.

Nancy compared the note to each name on the list. Finally she found a match.

"Bess, George," Nancy said. "The volunteer

who wrote the note was that kid Rusty!"

"Did somebody say my name?" a voice asked.

The girls whirled around. Rusty was standing behind them. He was holding a leash in one hand and a bag of dog poop in the other.

"I was just walking Champ," Rusty said.

"We can see that," George said, wrinkling her nose.

"Rusty, did you write this?" Nancy asked, holding up the taped-together note.

"Here. Hold this," Rusty said. He handed Nancy the poop bag and took the note.

Nancy scrunched her nose as she looked down at the bag. Rusty studied the note. He nodded and said, "Yeah. I wrote this. So what?"

"It's not nice to leave creepy notes around!" Bess scolded.

"I know, I know," Rusty said. "But that Maya was making fun of shelter dogs. And shelter dogs are great!"

"Is that why you switched Lola's biscuits, too?" Nancy asked.

"No way!" Rusty said. "That would be going against the Bow-Wow Brigade Pledge."

"What pledge?" George asked.

Rusty spun around. Printed on the back of his T-shirt was the Bow-Wow Brigade Pledge. The first line read, "Never hurt or trick any dog."

"A pledge is a serious promise," George whispered.

"I took a pledge," Bess said. "When I joined the Pixie Scouts."

"Well?" Rusty said, turning around. "Now do you believe me?"

"I guess so," Nancy said.

"But what is Maya's secret?" Bess asked.

Rusty tossed the orange note on the desk. Then he flashed a sly grin. "It's not nice to tell secrets, either," he said. "Come on, Champ. Let's go."

The girls watched as Rusty walked away.

"Wait!" Nancy called. "You forgot your bag!"

"Now we'll never know Maya's secret," George said.

"And now Nicki is our only suspect," added Bess.

"Maybe, maybe not," Nancy said. She tossed the bag into a trash can. Then she flipped the pages of the sign-in sheet until she found the one from Saturday.

"Look!" Nancy said. She pointed to a name near the bottom of the list. "Nicki Weidemeyer," she read. "That's got to be the Nicki we know."

"So Nicki *was* telling the truth," George said. "She really did volunteer with the dogs on Saturday."

"Now we have no suspects," Bess said. "And everyone still thinks we switched the dog biscuits."

The girls left the shelter. On their way out they ran into Mayor Strong.

"Hi, Mayor Strong," Nancy said. "What are you doing here?"

"I'm on my way to the vet stationed here," Mayor Strong said. "To pick up a special toothpaste for my dog Huey."

"What makes it special?" George asked.

"It's superstrong," the mayor said. "Huey has had the worst dog breath since Saturday. Sort of like cheese and onions!"

"Cheese and onions?" said Nancy.

Mayor Strong nodded. "Now if I can just get Huey to stop drooling like Niagara Falls," he muttered.

The girls said goodbye as the mayor entered the building.

"Wasn't the flavor of Lola's favorite dog biscuits cheese and onion?" George asked.

"Mayor Strong said Huey's breath has been stinky since Saturday," Nancy said.

"The day of the fashion show!" Bess gasped.

Nancy smiled as the pieces in her mind began to click together.

"Maybe Lola's biscuits weren't switched," she said. "Maybe they were *eaten*!"

# ChaPTER NINE

## "Newfie . . . Goofy!"

"You mean Huey ate Lola's dog biscuits?" Bess asked.

Nancy nodded and said, "There were no crumbs, remember? A big dog like Huey could have eaten those biscuits in one gulp!"

"And when the basket was empty," George said, "Peter might have replaced them with the dog biscuits he had in his pocket."

"Which could have been Lick My Chops!" Nancy put in.

"But why wouldn't Peter say anything?" Bess asked. "He saw how everyone was blaming us."

"Because Huey is the mayor's dog," Nancy said. "And Peter was responsible for him."

"Maybe he was afraid to let anyone know," said George.

Nancy remembered how nervous Peter had acted in the school yard. No wonder he didn't want to talk about Huey!

"I do think Huey ate the biscuits," Nancy said. "But before we accuse him, we have to do a little research."

"Research on what?" George asked.

"On dogs!" Nancy replied with a smile.

The Clue Crew raced to their headquarters. George found a website about different dog breeds. They couldn't remember the type of dog Huey was, but they remembered what he looked like.

"That's him!" Nancy said. She pointed to a big black dog on the screen.

"That's a Newfoundland," Bess said, reading carefully. "Newfie for short."

"It says they used to help fishermen pull in their nets," George went on. "And that they love water."

"It also says Newfies drool in long, sticky ropes," Nancy added.

"Can you imagine having a dog like that?" said Bess. "He probably drools on everything—furniture, the floor—"

"The floor!" Nancy said. "Maybe that's what that sticky puddle in Lola's trailer was."

"You mean that was Huey's drool?" Bess asked. She scrunched up her nose. "What else does it say about Eww-fies, I mean, Newfies?"

George read out loud: "Newfies' coats have long black hairs. They shed often, too."

"I wonder if Huey left hairs in the trailer too," Nancy said.

"Wonder no more!" exclaimed Bess.

"Huh?" George said.

Bess ran to her jacket. She pulled her Hairy Fairy Wand from her pocket.

"I used this right after we were in Lola's trailer, remember?" Bess said. "Huey's hairs could be on it."

The Clue Crew examined the sticky white

tape on the
Hairy Fairy.
There were lots
of light hairs—
just like Lola's.
There were also long,
thick black hairs—just
like Huey's!

"Maya and her parents have blond hair," said Nancy. "So the black hairs must be Huey's!"

"Good work, Gizmo Girl!" George said.

"Thanks!" Bess said.

"Let's question our new suspect," Nancy suggested. "Peter Patino."

Nancy found Peter Patino's address in the River Heights Elementary School yearbook. It was three blocks away.

When the girls reached the Patino house,

they found Peter in his front yard. Huey was also in the yard. He was sitting in a plastic kiddie pool, covered with soapsuds!

"Peter's giving Huey a bath," Bess whispered. "It's a good thing Newfies like water."

Peter stopped scrubbing as the girls walked over.

"Hi, Peter," Nancy said. "Hi, Huey."

The girls stepped back as Huey panted.

His dog breath *was* pretty funky!

"Mayor Strong asked me to wash Huey," said Peter. "It took four dog biscuits to get him into the bath."

"What kind of dog biscuits?" Nancy asked. "Lick My Chops . . . or Bone Appetit?"

Peter froze with his hands on Huey's wet coat. "I don't remember," he said. "Dog biscuits are dog biscuits."

"Not to Lola," George said. "Did Huey eat her fancy biscuits before the fashion show?"

"Nuh-uh," Peter said, shaking his head.

Nancy didn't always like tricking suspects

into confessing. But sometimes it was the only thing to do. . . .

"First Huey ate the biscuits," Nancy said. "Then he got muddy paw prints all over Lola's fancy dog bed. And after that, he ripped up some of Lola's clothes. Right?"

"Wrong!" Peter exclaimed. "All Huey did was eat those stinky dog biscuits—"

Peter clapped his wet hand over his mouth. A bubble floated out between his fingers.

"Tell us what happened, Peter," said Nancy.

Peter uncovered his mouth. Then he took a long, deep breath.

"After I saw you on Saturday, Huey dragged me into Lola's trailer," he said. "He's so strong that I couldn't hold him back—even when he started eating the biscuits from the basket!"

"*All* the biscuits?" Bess asked.

"To the last crumb!" Peter said. "I didn't know what to do, so I refilled the basket with my own dog biscuits. How was I supposed to know that Lola hated Lick My Chops?"

"Why didn't you tell someone?" George asked. "You saw how everyone blamed us."

"I was in charge of Huey," Peter said. "So when he goofed, I didn't want anyone to know. Especially since he's the mayor's dog. I'm sorry!"

"It wasn't your fault," said Bess. "Dogs will be dogs."

"You should tell Maya what you just told us, Peter," Nancy said. "Then maybe she'll stop blaming us for switching the biscuits."

"And start blaming me?" Peter said. "I don't think so!"

Huey barked. He jumped out of the pool and began shaking the water off his thick, wet coat. The girls and Peter screamed as they got showered.

"I think Huey is trying to tell you something," Nancy said.

Peter brushed back his wet hair with his hand. "Okay," he said. "Let's get this over with!"

Peter had seen Lola's trailer on River Street after school. When the kids reached River Street, it was still there.

"There's Maya!" Nancy said.

Maya and her mom were walking out of a pet photography studio. Maya held Lola's leash while her mom stopped to buy coffee from a cart.

"Maya!" called Nancy.

"Leave us alone," Maya called back. She walked Lola into the trailer. Nancy, Bess, George, and Peter followed them inside.

"I said leave us alone!" Maya warned.

"It's okay, Maya," Nancy said gently. "Peter Patino was at the park on Saturday. He has something to tell you."

"What?" Maya asked.

"We-ell," Peter started. He shuffled his feet. "It's sort of . . . like this . . . you see . . ."

George gave Peter a nudge with her elbow.

"Mayor Strong's dog, Huey, ate Lola's fancy dog biscuits," Peter blurted out. "While I was walking him."

"He did?" gasped Maya.

"I couldn't stop him," Peter said. "I'm sorry."

"Wow," Maya said. She looked at Nancy, Bess, and George. "So you didn't switch the biscuits. The mayor's dog ate them?"

"Yes," Nancy said.

Maya gave a little snort. "That sounds like something a dumb shelter dog would do. They're nothing but trouble."

Nancy frowned. She was glad the Bow-Wow Brigade wasn't around to hear that!

"I guess I'm sorry for blaming you," Maya

told the girls. "But you'd better go now. Lola has another photo shoot in exactly ten minutes."

"I'm outta here!" Peter declared. In a flash he was out of the trailer.

"We'd better go too," Nancy said.

Maya turned to Lola. She began brushing her coat with a silver-plated hairbrush.

The girls headed toward the door. Nancy glanced at Lola's puppy picture on the wall. It showed Maya holding a tiny white poodle in her arms. Nancy remembered seeing it when they were in the trailer before.

*Cute!* she thought.

She was about to follow Bess and George when she noticed something else. In the picture was a crate—the cardboard kind used to bring puppies and kittens home for the first time. Nancy wondered if the writing on the crate was in French, since Maya said that Lola was from France. But the print was too small to read.

*My spyglass!* Nancy remembered. She reached into her pocket and pulled it out.

"What are you doing, Nancy?" whispered Bess.

Nancy peered through the spyglass as she read the words silently to herself: "Valley View Pet Shelter. Next Stop: Home!"

"Bess, George!" Nancy gasped. "I think I just found out Maya's secret!"

# CHAPTER TEN

## Happily Ever After

Nancy held the spyglass as Bess and George looked through it. They read the words to themselves.

"Wow!" Bess said.

"No wonder Rusty knew Lola's secret," George whispered. "He volunteered at the Valley View Shelter!"

"What are you doing?" Maya called.

The girls turned to Maya.

"Question," Nancy said. "Is Lola a shelter dog?"

Maya froze with the hairbrush in her hand. Then she shook her head. "Shelter dog?" she scoffed. "Ha, ha, very funny."

"Then what's a shelter crate doing in Lola's puppy picture?" Nancy asked.

Maya's eyes popped open wide. She glanced at the picture and shook her head.

"The puppy in the picture isn't Lola," she said. "That's some Lola wannabe from the Valley View Shelter. We were giving her diva lessons and . . . and . . . and . . ."

Nancy folded her arms across

her chest. Maya's voice cracked as she tried again.

"I needed a crate for an arts and crafts project," Maya said quickly. "So I went to the Valley View Shelter and . . . and . . . and . . ."

Maya's eyes darted around the room. They finally landed on Nancy.

"Okay." Maya sighed. "My parents adopted Lola as a puppy at the Valley View Shelter. So I guess that does make her a—"

Maya gulped hard. She opened her mouth, but all that came out was a squeak.

"Go ahead. Say it," Nancy said gently.

"THAT MAKES HER A SHELTER DOG!" Maya blurted. "There! Are you happy now?"

Lola began licking Maya's face.

"Somebody seems to be," Nancy giggled.

"But why was it such a big secret?" Bess asked.

"Yeah," George said. "Adopting homeless dogs is a great thing."

"It started when Lola got famous," Maya

said. "I didn't think anyone would buy calendars and cards from a shelter dog. So I made up a fancy story to go with Lola's fancy life. I begged my parents to go along with it and they did."

Tears filled Maya's eyes as she petted Lola.

"Lola may be a French poodle," Maya sniffed. "But she's never even been to France. Not even to Paris, Texas!"

Maya buried her face in Lola's coat. She began to sob loudly.

"Don't cry, Maya," Nancy said. "Lola's story is even better now!"

"It is?" asked Maya. Her voice sounded muffled through Lola's fur.

"Sure," Nancy said. "Most people don't know you can adopt purebred dogs at shelters. Or puppies that can grow up to become superstars, just like Lola!"

Maya choked back the tears as she looked up.

"Don't you see, Maya?" Nancy went on excitedly. "Lola is just like Cinderella!"

"I get it!" George said. "It's like she went from wags . . . to riches!"

This time even Bess laughed at George's dog joke.

"Lola the Cinderella Dog!" Maya declared. She nodded her head. "I like it. I like it."

"So do I," Nancy told Bess and George. "Not only is Lola's secret out—but the Clue Crew solved another case!"

"It's just like a fairy tale!" Bess swooned.

Nancy, Bess, and George stood outside the Rollover Rescue Shelter. They gazed at Lola, dressed in a white lace doggy gown and silver tiara. She made the perfect Cinderella—and the perfect poster pup for Adopt-a-Shelter-Dog Day!

While the Bow-Wow Brigade walked adoptable dogs, Maya chatted with a news reporter.

"Is it true?" the reporter asked. "Did Lola the Diva Dog really come from a shelter?"

"Oh, yes!" Maya said. She looked straight

into the camera. "I guess you can say she went from wags to riches!"

"That was my joke," George muttered.

Peter came over with Huey on a leash. Nancy couldn't believe her eyes. Instead of pulling Peter, the big Newfie was walking calmly at his side!

"What happened to Huey?" asked George.

"When I told Mayor Strong about Huey and the biscuits, he decided to send him to obedience school," Peter explained. "Now Huey is an A student!"

"Way to go, Huey!" Nancy cheered. She jumped back before Huey could drool on her sneaker.

"Nancy, Bess, George!" a voice called.

Nancy turned. It was Nicki, walking a small pointy-eared dog on a leash.

"Look at my new dog!" exclaimed Nicki.

"I thought you couldn't have a dog because of your allergic brother," Nancy said.

"No problem," said Nicki. "Meet Enrique—a Mexican hairless!"

"I never met a bald dog before," Bess said.

"No hair, no sneeze!" explained Nicki.

"Wow!" George said. "I guess there is a dog out there for everyone."

Next came the moment the girls had been waiting for. Vincent, dressed like a fairy tale prince, got down on one knee as he fitted Lola with a crystal-clear doggy shoe.

"Glass slippers can be bought at the Funky Fido Boutique," Patsy Ray announced. "Get a pair for your princess pup while supplies last!"

Nancy turned to smile at her best friends. "This fairy tale had a happy ending," she said. "Thanks to the Clue Crew!"

"I guess we are good detectives," Bess said.

"Are you kidding?" George said with a grin. "We're *doggone* good!"

# Say Fleas!

Who says only divas get star treatment? Now your fave dog or top cat can get face time with their own picture frame, made and designed by YOU!

## You Will Need:

One picture of your pet
Acrylic paint
Fine-tipped marker
Arts and crafts glue
Paint brush
5-x-7-inch piece of plain
   cardboard
Pair of scissors or craft
   knife
Clear nail polish
Ribbon or magnet

## On Your Bark . . . Get Set . . . Go!

Place the picture of your pet in the center of the cardboard, and use a pencil to trace around the picture. Ask an adult to help you cut out a hole for the picture.

Glue dog biscuits or any solid pet treats to the frame. Add stickers, glitter, feathers—even your pet's paw print for extra pizzazz!

Use the marker to write your pet's name on one of the treats, then brush clear nail polish over the treats for a shiny finish.

When its dry, flip the frame over and glue your pet's picture on the back.

Glue a magnet or colorful ribbon on the back of the frame.

Wait for the glue to dry, then hang up and enjoy!

Don't forget—frames can be for the birds, too! Decorate a frame with jingly bells and colorful bird seed. It's sure to fly with your best feathered friend.

You always knew your pet was perfect. Now he's picture perfect!!

Read all the books in the

# Blast to the Past

series!

#1 Lincoln's Legacy

#2 Disney's Dream

#3 Bell's Breakthrough

#4 King's Courage

#5 Sacagawea's Strength

#6 Ben Franklin's Fame

#7 Washington's War

Coming Soon:

#8 Betsy's Star

Calling all detectives, junior sleuths, and mystery lovers...

NANCY DREW AND THE CLUE CREW™

# Need Your Help!

Visit

## NANCY DREW AND THE CLUE CREW CLUB

at www.SimonSaysSleuth.com

Membership is **FREE** and you will enjoy:

- contests and sweepstakes -
- fun quizzes -
- exciting mysteries -
- official club news -

and much more!

*Visit www.SimonSaysSleuth.com today.*

Solve mysteries! Find clues! Have fun!